Time to Say Bye-Bye
Hora de Dizer Tchau-Tchau

Maryann Cocca-Leffler

Bab'l Books

To Uncle Richie and Aunt Linda,
to share with your grandchildren.
Love, Maryann

Previously Published in 2012 by Viking- Penguin Group, Inc

Translation Copyright © 2016 by Babl Books, Inc. Provo, UT

Translations provided by the Babl Books Community, with
final editing by Vanessa B. Frye.

Bilingual edition published by Babl Books, Inc.
www.bablbooks.com

ISBN 978-1-68304-053-8

Busy, busy day! Time to go...

Dia ocupado, ocupado! Hora de ir...

to the park.

para o parque.

Swinging,

Balançando,

digging,

cavando,

riding fun.

passeando de carro,

me divertindo.

I don't want to leave.

Eu não quero ir embora.

But it's
time to say
bye-bye.

Mas é
hora de dizer
tchau-tchau.

Bye-bye swing.
Tchau-tchau balanço.

Bye-bye sandbox.
Tchau-tchau caixa de areia.

Bye-bye friend.

Tchau-tchau amiga.

Time to go...

Hora de...

to Grandma's.
ir para a casa da vovó.

Dancing,

Dançando,

baking,

cozinhando,

smelling flowers.

cheirando flores.

I want
to stay.

Eu quero
ficar.

But it's time to say bye-bye.

Mas é hora de dizer tchau-tchau.

Bye-bye
cookies.

Tchau-tchau
biscoitos.

Bye-bye flowers.

Tchau-tchau flores.

Bye-bye Grandma.

Tchau-tchau vovó.

Time to go...

Hora de...

back
home.

voltar
para casa.

Eating,

Comendo,

building,
construindo,

toy parade.

desfile de brinquedo.

I'm still playing.
Eu ainda estou brincando.

But it's time to say bye-bye.
Mas é hora de dizer tchau-tchau.

Bye-bye dishes.

Tchau-tchau louças.

Bye-bye blocks.

Tchau-tchau blocos.

Bye-bye toys.

Tchau-tchau brinquedos.

Time to go...

Hora de...

bubble hair.

cabelo com bolhas.

I'm not done yet.

Eu ainda não acabei.

But it's time to say bye-bye.

Mas é hora de dizer tchau-tchau.

Bye-bye bath.

Tchau-tchau banheira.

Bye-bye boat.

Tchau-tchau barco.

Bye-bye ducky.

Tchau-tchau pato.

Because...

Porque...

it's bedtime.
é hora de
ir para a cama.

Reading stories
and more stories,

Lendo histórias e
mais histórias,

cozy cuddles.

abraços
carinhosos.

I'm not sleepy.

Eu não estou com sono.

But it's time to say night-night.

Mas é hora de dizer boa-noite.

Night-night light.
Boa noite luz.

Night-night books.
Boa noite livros.

Night-night Mommy.
Boa noite mamãe.

Time for...
Hora de...

sweet dreams!

sonhos doces!

Made in the USA
San Bernardino, CA
26 November 2018